Mr. Owliver's Magic at the Museum

Written and Illustrated
by Carolyn Bracken

4880 Lower Valley Road • Atglen, PA 19310

To Henry, who I fell in love with when
I caught him teary-eyed in front of a Van Gogh.

~ Carolyn Bracken

"The Loge"
Auguste
Wrenoir

Mr. Owliver loved his job.

He was night watchman at the Animaltown Art Museum, and—as an owl—being around beautiful things all night long suited him fine.

His duty was to protect the masterpieces. He was proud to do that.

When Mr. Owliver got to work each evening, he would say, "Goodnight" to the day crew and, "Hello" to the cleaning crew, then he would make his rounds.

He liked being able to get up close to the paintings that people stood in long lines to see, paintings like the "Mona Lizard,"

"Mona Lizard"

Leonardo DaVinci

or Grant Woodchuck's "American Gothic."

"American
Gothic"

Grant Woodchuck

No daytime crowds or lines for Mr. Owliver!

He patrolled the long hallways saying hello to "Piggie" and the "Blue Bird,"

"Piggie"
Thomas Lawrence

"Bluebird"
Thomas Gainesborough

and the couple in Jan Van Duck's "The Marriage Portrait."

They always seemed happy to see him.

Just before midnight he would let the cleaning crew out, then go to his office to fetch his lunch box.

He had a favorite lunch spot, the bench in front of "The Loge" by Auguste Wrenoir. He liked to look at the lovely lady wren in the painting.

She always seemed to look back at him.
Though Mr. Owliver didn't much like her male companion.

His friends would often ask if being a night watchman was a lonely job.

ANNO·ETATIS·

·SVÆ·XLIX·

Hans Bovine

"Henry the Ape"

How was that possible when he could have such interesting conversations with "Henry the Ape,"

and Vincent Van Goat's "Dr. Goatchet" anytime he wished?

He could watch the dancers in Henri Catisse's painting,
or Edgar Dogas's "The Dancing Class,"

"Dancers III"
Henri Catisse

"The Dancing Class"
Edgar Dogas

George Sir Rat

"Sunday in
the Park"

or take a stroll in George Sir Rat's sunny riverside park.

Before he knew it, the day crew was filing in through the
museum's entrance.

As everyone else began their jobs,
        Mr. Owliver headed home for dinner and bed.

The following night was Mr. Owliver's birthday. He stopped at the bakery to buy himself something special for his midnight lunch. He was looking forward to sharing it with the lovely Miss Wren.

After making his rounds and saying goodnight to the cleaning crew, Mr. Owliver got his lunch box and walked the long hallway to Miss Wren's gallery.

But something didn't feel quite right. He decided he was just hungry and excited to eat his birthday treat.

Mr. Owliver reached his favorite spot, opened his lunch box, and began chatting away to Miss Wren. But, when he took his birthday cupcake out to show her, he looked up at the painting and . . . .

She wasn't **there!** And neither was her **companion!**

Where were they?!

"Adoration
of the Mag Pie"
Bermese Luini

"Sow before a Mirror"
Pablo Pigasso

"Aristotle with the
Bust of Homer"

Rembrant
Rin Tin Tin

Then he noticed that the Sow in Pablo Pigasso's
painting wasn't standing before her mirror, and the Magpies in
"The Adoration" had all flown away, and Rembrandt Rin Tin Tin's
bust of Homer was missing his Aristotle! They had all disappeared!

George Sir Rat

"Sunday in the Park"

He was supposed to protect the masterpieces, and he had failed at his job.

Suddenly, he heard faint music coming from the last gallery, the one far down the hall. Its doors were shut tight. But when Mr. Owliver pulled them open . . .

. . . the lights popped on to the cries of,
"Surprise!" and **"Happy Birthday!"**

There were all his friends: The Woodchucks, Mona Lizard, The Newlyweds, Blue Bird, Piggie, Dr. Goatchet, Henry the Ape, The Dancing Cats and Dogs, the Rats from the park, the Sow, Aristotle, and The Magpies. Best of all, standing beside a big birthday cake and a pile of presents was Miss Wren.

"Happy Birthday, Mr. Owliver," she said as she shyly handed him a big slice of cake.

She introduced him to her companion—who turned out to be her brother and not such a bad fellow after all.

Dr. Goatchet put on music, and Mr. Owliver asked Miss Wren if she would like to dance. She said she'd be delighted, and they danced and danced the night away.

It was the best and strangest birthday
Mr. Owliver ever had.

A masterpiece of a birthday.

With admiration, and apologies, to the original artists & their masterpieces.

The *Mona Lisa* was painted on a simple slab of poplar wood and has been described as the most famous painting in the world.

Find it at:
The Louvre, Paris

MONA LISA, 1502–05
Leonardo Da Vinci, 1452–1519

Though she looks older, the girl in the painting is only eleven years old.

Find it at:
The Huntington, Los Angeles

PINKIE, 1794
Thomas Lawrence, 1769–1830

Wood's original inspiration for the painting was the house placed behind the farmer couple.

Find it at:
Art Institute Chicago

AMERICAN GOTHIC, 1930
Grant Wood, 1891–1942

The Blue Boy and *Pinkie* are GFFs—gallery friends forever. In real life they hang on opposite walls from each other.

Find it at:
The Huntington, Los Angeles

BLUE BOY, 1770
Sir Thomas Gainsborough, 1727–1788

Art critics believe that the artist himself is shown in the circular mirror behind the couple.

Find it at:
National Gallery, London

THE WEDDING PORTRAIT, 1434
Jan Van Eyck, 1390–1441

"La Loge" means "The Opera Box." This was a favorite subject for modern-thinking painters in the late 1800s, as it was a place where the rich and poor intermingled.

Find it at:
Courtauld Gallery, London

THE LOGE, 1874
Pierre Auguste Renoir, 1841–1919

The original painting was destroyed by fire in 1698. But long before that Henry had it copied many times by other artists to give as a gift.

Find it at:
Galleria Nazionale d'Arte Antica, Rome

HENRY THE EIGHTH, 1540
Hans Holbein, 1497–1543

Dr. Paul Gachet cared for Vincent's physical as well as emotional health.

Private Collection, Tokyo
Find the second version at:
Musee d'Orsay, Paris

DOCTOR GACHET, 1890
Vincent Van Gogh, 1853–1890

Art critics believe that the figure at the bottom (nearest the viewer) has stumbled during the circle dance.

Find it at:
The Hermitage, St. Petersburg, Russia

DANCERS III, 1910
Henri Matisse, 1869–1954

Those are the young dancers' mothers observing the class in the upper right corner of the painting.

Find it at:
The Metropolitan Museum, NYC

THE DANCING CLASS II, 1874
Edgar Degas, 1834–1917

It took Seurat two whole years to complete the painting.

Find it at:
Art Institute Chicago

A SUNDAY AFTERNOON ON THE ISLAND OF LA GRANDE JATTE, 1886
Georges Seurat, 1859–1891

Everybody's clothing in the painting has traveled through time. The fashions are what people in medieval times would wear.

Find it at:
The Louvre, Paris

ADORATION OF THE MAGI, 1520–1525
Bernadino Luini, 1480–1532

The yellow half of the girl's face stands for her youthful and happy times. The dark colors in that part of her reflection tell of a fear of losing her beauty and getting older.

Find it at:
Museum of Modern Art, NYC

GIRL BEFORE A MIRROR, 1932
Pablo Picasso, 1881–1973

Some art critics believe the painting suggests that the rich and famous philosopher, Aristotle, really envied the simple, humble life of the blind poet, Homer.

Find it at:
The Metropolitan Museum, NYC

ARISTOTLE WITH A BUST OF HOMER, 1653
Rembrandt Van Rijn, 1606–1669

Art History Timeline

Renaissance
1300–1600 AD

Baroque
1650 AD

Rococo
1750 AD

Impressionism
1850 AD

Post Impressionism
1880 AD

Fauvism
1900 AD

Modernism
1930 AD

Cubism
1910 AD

Other Schiffer Books on Related Subjects:

Change the World Before Bedtime, Mark Kimball Moulton, Josh Chalmers, and Karen Good, 978-0-7643-4238-7
I Hate Picture Books!, Timothy Young, 978-0-7643-4387-2
The Future Architect's Tool Kit, Barbara Beck, 978-0-7643-5193-8

Text & Illustrations Copyright © 2017 by Carolyn Bracken

Library of Congress Control Number: 2017935609

Designed by Danielle D. Farmer
Type set in Love Letters/Book Antiqua

ISBN: 978-0-7643-5427-4
Printed in China

Co-published by Pixel Mouse House &
Schiffer Publishing, Ltd.
4880 Lower Valley Road
Atglen, PA 19310
Phone: (610) 593-1777; Fax: (610) 593-2002
E-mail: Info@schifferbooks.com
Web: www.schifferbooks.com

For our complete selection of fine books on this and related subjects,
please visit our website at www.schifferbooks.com. You may also write for a free catalog.

Schiffer Publishing's titles are available at special discounts for bulk purchases for sales promotions or premiums. Special editions, including personalized covers, corporate imprints, and excerpts, can be created in large quantities for special needs. For more information, contact the publisher.

We are always looking for people to write books on new and related subjects.
If you have an idea for a book, please contact us at proposals@schifferbooks.com.